It is a strange and difficult time we are in this age of Covid-19. Schools are clo[sed,] some parks are even closed. Everywhe[re,] most people are not able to visit their f[riends or] their family that they don't live with. No[t doing what] we usually do, or go where we want at [... is] the question I keep asking myself. I am curious to ask you too....

Just Supposing...

you woke up tomorrow
and there weren't all these rules
like: YOU HAVE TO STAY HOME!
and: YOU CAN'T GO TO SCHOOL!
And whatever you wished for,
where to go, what to do,
who to be with, how many –
was all up to you.
Where would it be,
doing what, and with whom?
Would you go to the park
or fly up to the moon?
You could go on a picnic
or stay in your room.
If you woke up tomorrow,
restrictions all lifted –
what kind of a world
would you want to be gifted?

Copyright © Cheryl Moskowitz 2020
www.cherylmoskowitz.com

First published in Great Britain in 2020
by Circle Time Press
www.circletimepress.co.uk

All rights reserved

No part of this publication may be reproduced, stored in a retrieval system, or transmitted, in any form, or by any means, electrical, mechanical, photocopying, recording or otherwise without the prior written permission of the publisher or a licence permitting restricted copying. In the United Kingdom such licences are issued by the Copyright Licensing Agency, 5th Floor, Shackleton House, 4 Battle Bridge Lane, London, SE1 2HX. www.cla.co.uk

A catalogue record for this book is available
from the British Library

ISBN 978-0-9564082-6-6

Printed and bound by
Enfield Council Design & Print Services

THE CORONA COLLECTION

a conVerseation

CHERYL MOSKOWITZ

designed by Alastair Gavin

Contents

1	Just Supposing...
5	Introduction
6	School Rules!
7	School Trip
9	Coronasaurus
10	Back To Pen And Paper
11	A Wheelbarrow Full Of Ice Cream
12	Boredom
13	Not Alone
14	In These Coronavirus Times
15	Jamie Teaches Dylan His ABCs
16	Betty's Place
17	Arthur's Arms
18	Super, Secret, Special Sense
19	Betty's Secret
20	From Your Librarian During Lockdown
22	B's Bakery At The Wyatt Hotel
24	Easter On Lockdown
25	Moore's Millions
26	Key Worker
28	If I Could Go Anywhere?
31	Just For Now
32	New Blades
33	Oh No
34	Who Makes History?
36	Fantasy Football
37	Isn't It Odd
38	Care Taker
39	Kennings For Nicola
41	Animal Bonanza
43	Diary Of William
44	Have You Washed Your Hands?
46	What Is The Best Thing About Coming To School During Lockdown?
47	Daily Routine (A Tanka)
48	All It Takes Is A Little Thought
49	Colouring The Bricks
50	Life Lessons From A Teacher
51	SpaceX
51	Sharon's Sky At Night
52	When I Am Well Again
55	Round The Clock Song
56	Unicorn Magic
58	Virtually There
60	The Show Must Go On
62	Perfect Day
63	Making A Meal Of Pizza
64	Ahoy There, A Word From Your Captain
66	J'Ziah's Manifesto For The New World
68	Cocoon

Introduction

These are unprecedented times. The children who are living through the current pandemic will be writing the history books in the future.

Since schools closed in the UK except for children in special circumstances, I have felt an urgency to talk directly to children to find out what life is like for them in this age of Covid-19, and to reflect their perspectives through poetry.

I began by setting up pavement interviews – at a distance! – asking the question posed on the first page of this book. I continued the conversation in schools, conducting playground interviews with children and school staff.

Their responses have inspired these poems that will serve as a record of the time and I hope inspire continued conversation beyond the crisis.

A website, www.coronacollectionpoetry.com, has been created as a hub for information and resources relating to this project. The intention is also to collect your conversations as audio, video or text on this site, so please do visit!

Huge thanks are due to the children and families in my neighbourhood who have shared their thoughts with me; Carterhatch Junior School, and especially headteacher Helen McGovern for her support for this project; children and parents at Highfield Primary School; Alastair Gavin for a brilliant design; Martha Gavin for precise and insightful editing; and Kate McBarron for creative and energetic media coordination.

Finally, thank you to Dylan Calder and the team at Pop Up Projects, and Linda Stone at Enfield Council, for their generosity and commitment to the wide distribution of this pamphlet, and also their creative input into the accompanying resources.

Theo is in Year 4. He doesn't have much space at home and gets bored easily without something to do so he, for one, is glad that he can go into school for a few hours most days.

School Rules!

They've closed the park with the zipline
the playing fields and football pitch too.

It's frustrating, irritating
with nowhere to go, nothing to do.

Everything's shut, the swings, the slide
so I'm glad they've made it a rule

that instead of staying at home
I have to come into school, that's cool!

Tom is in Year 6 and was supposed to be going away before Easter with his class on their school trip. He'd been looking forward to it so was sad about not being able to go.

School Trip

We were supposed to be going to PGL
  it was cancelled
    We were going to Suffolk with our school
      now we're not going
        Everyone together, the whole Year 6
          no one can go
            To learn to make rafts with twine and sticks
              we'll never go now
                You have to find branches of similar lengths
                  we have to stay home
                    That's how you give the raft its strength
                      and not see friends
                        You need to find something to use as a buoy
                          find things to do
                            Could be an empty bottle or a plastic toy
                              till the virus ends
                                Tie it to the raft with a bowline knot
                                  could be ages
                                    Try it on the water, see what you've got!
                                      have to be patient
                                        If it sinks, don't worry, you can try other ways
                                          learn new things
                                            There's really no hurry, we've got all day!

...yet it is having a gigantic effect on the world. A 'monster' is something of extraordinary or daunting size. I think that the coronavirus has become the monster of our times. There have been other monsters throughout history that have been just as huge and scary. Most of these eventually became extinct or were defeated somehow. Think of the dinosaurs, Saint George and the Dragon, the Great Plague, the Fire of London...

Coronasaurus

Back in the Dark Ages, Yersinia Pestis
Took off with some rats on a merchant ship
Spreading the plague from Far East to Damascus
Grabbing hold of the world with its deadly grip.

And then came a spark from a baker's oven
Setting London ablaze with unstoppable flames.
It burned all the houses and with it, the vermin
The fleas and the pests they said were to blame.

And now comes the mighty Coronasaurus
With its terrible cough and invisible claws
With its feverish roar and insidious chorus
EVERYONE HAS TO STAY INDOORS!

Will we be extinct, or will it go before us?
Can we learn from this time while we're all stuck inside?
Is it right that this beast has the power to bore us
How can we stand by while so many die?

Here are some things I've learned from isolation
The sky is much bluer, the grass is more green
While staying at home is not quite a vacation
It's time to take stock, if you know what I mean.

An asteroid from space finished dinosaurs off
I'm not thinking of wishing on that kind of star
But with patience and kindness and that kind of stuff
We can battle this monster from right where we are!

Anna is in Year 8 at secondary school. She misses sitting around in a group at school chatting with her friends, and giving hugs whenever they see one another. She's trying to think up new ways to stay connected and close.

Dear friends,

I miss you!

Back To Pen And Paper

I'm trying to keep in touch with my friends
by writing letters and posting them.
It's better for me than talking online
this way I can be with them all of the time
so even when they go off screen
they're still right here if you get what I mean.
Of course, I miss us being together
but I hope that doesn't have to be forever
I like taking the time to write beautifully
using colours and shapes and calligraphy
I keep my friends' letters close to my heart
which is much much closer than two metres apart.
And one day when Covid-19 is forgotten
I'll still have all the letters you've written.

from Anna

One of Anna's best memories from primary school is the off-menu ice cream stand they had at her Year 6 Leavers' Disco. Imagine having as much as you want, whenever you want, for free!

A Wheelbarrow Full Of Ice Cream

If I could break the rules I'd go back to school
and see all my friends, that would be so cool

If I could go anywhere, without restriction,
I'd escape this crazy science fiction

If I could fast forward into the future
I'd put Covid-19 out to pasture

But seeing as how the world must change
let's stick with less cars and fewer planes

And on a day like today, it would be my dream
to have a whole wheelbarrow filled with ice cream!

Living in isolation can be boring. I've been trying to find a way to describe the feeling…

Photo: Lee Slabber/Caters News

Boredom

Endlessly inside
Like one hundred rainy days
How can I explain?

The other day a fly came into my kitchen. Normally I shoo flies away but it occurred to me that this fly might be bored and lonely too. At the moment I'm not allowed to have any other friends round to visit me at my house so I thought I'd let this fly stay.

Not Alone

How much gladder
am I
of this fly
that buzzes here
at my windowsill
Now instead
of being alone
this fly and I
can share a home

Jamie is in Year 5. He's finding it hard because normally he would be spending more time outside and get to see his dad as well as his mum. The best thing for Jamie about being at home is spending time with his baby brother, Dylan. He'd like to go on holiday with his dad.

In These Coronavirus Times

I'm finding it hard
I can't go outside
or spend time with my Dad
and now I can't see him
I'm taking it bad
if I could make magic
a perfect day, say
I'd ask my dad
to take me away
back to that theme park
next to the sea
and instead of a day
we could stay a whole week
Dad, if you're listening
let's make a plan
to get back together
as soon as we can

Jamie Teaches Dylan His ABCs

Always at home
Baby with blond hair
Chubby cheeks
Dylan, you love to dribble
Even when you play
Fat little arms
Gurgling all day
He's my brother
I love him

Photo by Bambi Corro on Unsplash

Betty who is 8 years old likes cats and her 4-year-old brother Arthur likes pretending to be a rocketship and blasting off into space. He has enough energy to get there!

They share an ordinary size house, and a galaxy-sized imagination.

Betty's Place

If I was in a corona-free world,
I'd have special powers and fly
I'd zoom out into the universe
to a special place in the sky

There's another earth out there, you know
where people with special powers go
We all have powers within us, see?
There's a special place for you and me.

I'll have my super boots, Arthur has his gun
(Not the kind that kills, the kind that's fun)
He can use it to blast us to outer space
up to the sky, to Betty's Place.

It's a virus-free world, this new universe
where people get better (they never get worse)
and cats are the rulers because of their senses
they can jump over walls and climb over fences.

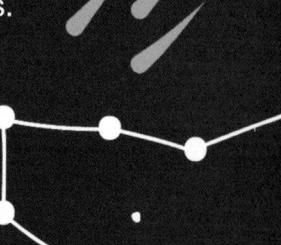

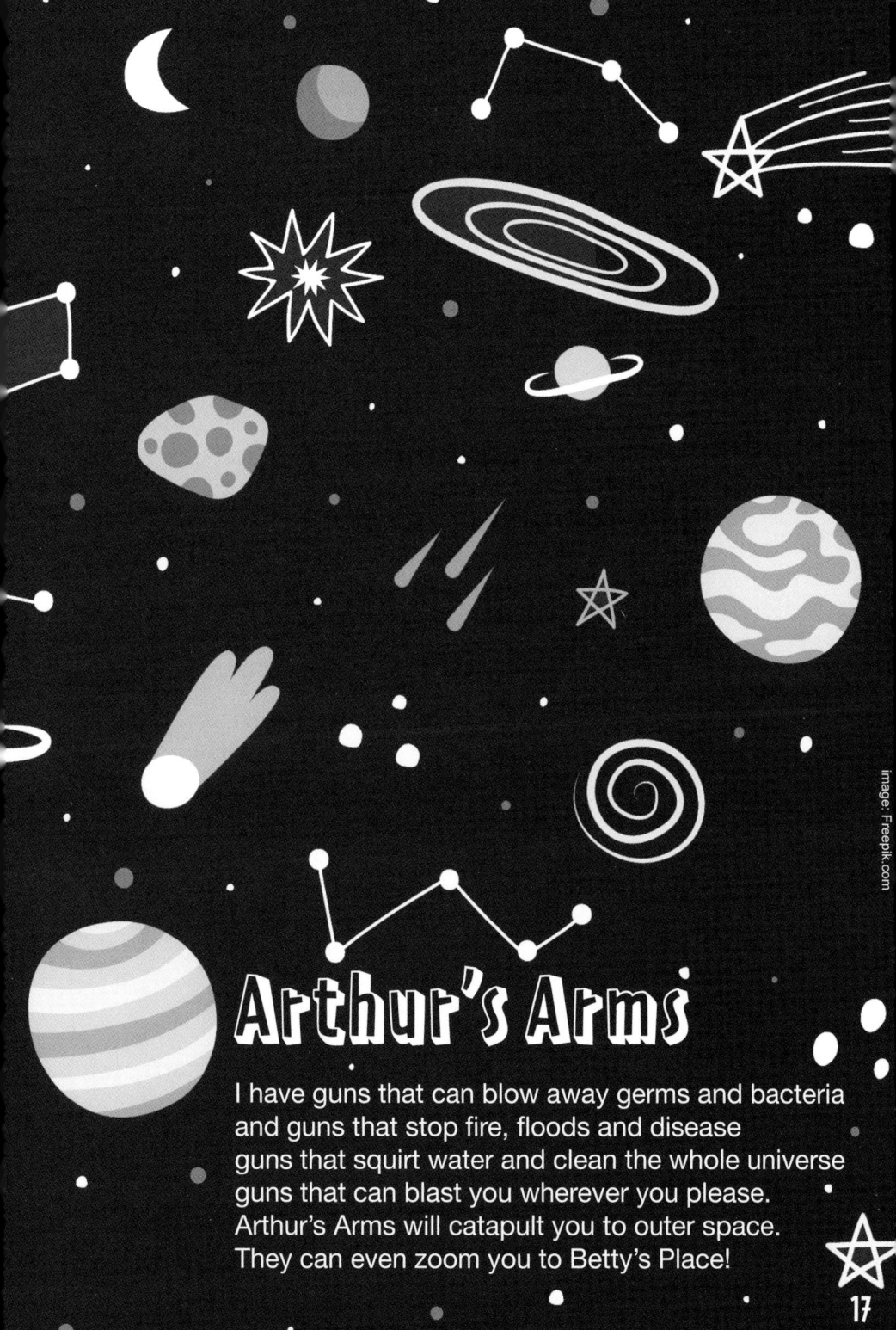

Arthur's Arms

I have guns that can blow away germs and bacteria
and guns that stop fire, floods and disease
guns that squirt water and clean the whole universe
guns that can blast you wherever you please.
Arthur's Arms will catapult you to outer space.
They can even zoom you to Betty's Place!

Super, Secret, Special Sense

Betty's super boots
Betty's secret world
Betty's special powers
Betty's sense of smell
Betty's super sensible, special secret:
THE FUTURE IS CATS!!!

Betty's Secret

I'll tell you a secret (but please don't tell)
I have a super-duper sense of smell
I can sleep for absolutely ages as well
I can see in the dark, even with my eyes closed
and when someone is near me, I always know!
I purr when I'm happy but I hiss when I'm mad
I know it sounds odd but just ask my Dad –
he'll tell you that I am really part cat (but don't tell!)

From Your Librarian During Lockdown

During the lockdown…

I still came to work every day
made new displays
recorded stories
and found new ways
to reach all of you staying at home

it felt safe to be in the library
with only stories
for company
though really quite eerie
not to be chatting about books I love

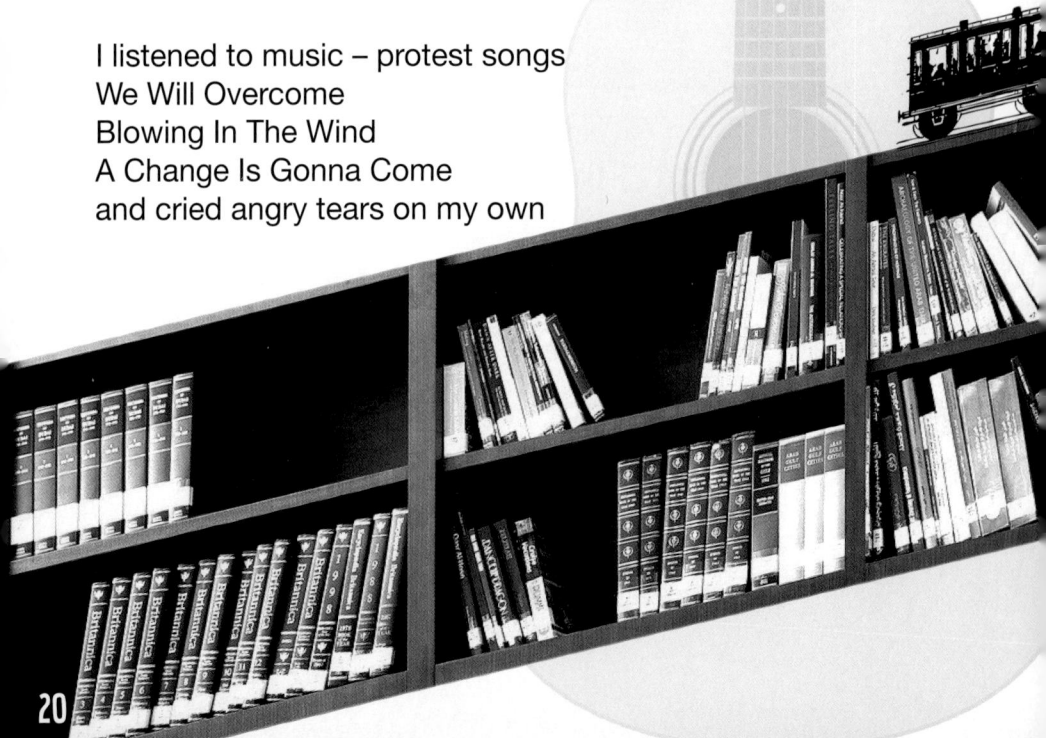

I listened to music – protest songs
We Will Overcome
Blowing In The Wind
A Change Is Gonna Come
and cried angry tears on my own

lessons on Zoom were surreal
seeing your names
but not your faces
was not ideal
but your responses made me incredibly happy

the best thing about coming back is the laughter
having conversations
in the same room
not just on Zoom
and discovering how to be safe, and together

when I was young my mother told me stories
about troubled times
and broken-down trains
I memorised lines
like that one from *The Little Engine That Could*

I won't let Covid-19 stop me having my dream
that by sharing words
from stories we've heard
we can change the world
I think we can, I think we can… I know we will.

Wyatt is 7 and Bella is 9. Their dad is a football coach but right now his team has had to stop training and can't play matches. Wyatt and Bella are doing lots of exercising at home though, so maybe their dad has passed on some of his training tips to them instead!

Wyatt likes art and is especially good at drawing trees. Bella loves cooking and has been trying out lots of new recipes.

B's Bakery At The Wyatt Hotel

Wyatt's good at art, Bella's good at cooking.
They run this place together, why not make a booking?

Bella will make a gingerbread house,
a kind of factory that never runs out –
eat a door or a window, it'll come back again,
plenty more on the shelf… plus gingerbread men!
Outside it looks small, but inside it's huge –
endless gingerbread sweets for me and for you!

Wyatt's the manager of this five-star hotel,
with multi-screen cinema, popcorn as well.
The inside is plush with amazing décor.
From wall to ceiling on every floor,
paintings of cherry trees in full blossom.
Wyatt's own artwork – go there, it's awesome!

A house made of gingerbread, not bricks, wood or glass,
and a five-star hotel, that is really first class!
Bella likes finding new recipes too,
Wyatt is looking for drawings by you!

I sat on the pavement by Bella and Wyatt's front garden before Easter. It was full of Easter decorations.

Easter On Lockdown

So what are we doing at home every day,
while we're whiling this isolation away?
Gardening, playing, and being creative,
talking on the phone with millions of relatives!
Keeping fit and making an Easter display,
our garden's a real Easter Island today.

There's a strawberry house, decorated with eggs,
birds on branches and toadstools with legs!
Gnomes and fairies that live in tree houses,
bird-feeders with seeds, and cats chasing mouses.
Squirrels in the trees and a pixie standing guard,
he comes from Cornwall and has a big beard.
Even from the pavement, you'll have a good view:
this is Easter Island, Lockdown Avenue.

There have been lots of amazing stories about what people are doing to help one another during this crisis. One man called Thomas Moore walked up and down his garden 100 times in the run-up to his 100th birthday and raised over £30 million for the NHS.

Moore's Millions

When Captain Tom was ninety-nine
He walked one hundred laps
His fellow soldiers stood in line
The nation cheered and clapped.

Daisy, Charlie and Flo's mum is a physiotherapist. Normally she works in a small clinic but because of Covid-19 she has gone to work in the bigger hospitals to help look after patients suffering from the virus.

Charlie explained what it is like to have a mum who is a…

Key Worker

I was concerned when Mum said she had to go into Intensive Care, to help look after the people with the virus there, I couldn't be sure if they'd have enough gloves or gowns, or protective visors. And Mum likes biscuits when she has her tea but they don't even have enough PPE so they may not have any custard creams either. But all the biscuits in the world can't stop the people from getting ill or protect my mum from the sadness and crying when some of the people end up dying and all their families need my mum to keep up their spirits and try for them like she does for me, to tell them a joke or bring them tea and hold their hand for a while when they're scared in the night or sing that song about 'being alright' to make them smile. She does 12-hour shifts, sometimes more, sometimes longer. She gets more tired as the virus gets stronger. But I'm really quite proud if truth be told. I mean she's not that elderly or terribly old and her lungs are good and her heart's still beating and she likes the people she's been meeting and even though she hardly gets a break, she's just doing her job, for goodness sake!

The family were all supposed to be in Italy for Easter but their trip was cancelled because of the coronavirus.

Charlie said he didn't really mind not going anywhere right now, though he could think of lots of places he might like to visit one day, somehow…

If I Could Go Anywhere?

I'd start in the park right here with my friends
then maybe Australia and the Mediterranean
perhaps then to Italy, and Colorado too
to see bears at Yellowstone (not in a zoo!)

I'd go in a boat and not on a plane
I'd travel by bicycle, bus or train
we need more lanes for skates and scooters
better public transport for all the commuters

There are good things about not going anywhere
there's already less pollution and much cleaner air
in a short amount of time there is lots lots less
instead of school right now we can learn from this

When this is all over, what will I miss?
the quiet, the calm, the lack of busyness
the books, the conversations, the stories in my head
travelling in my dreams while staying in bed!

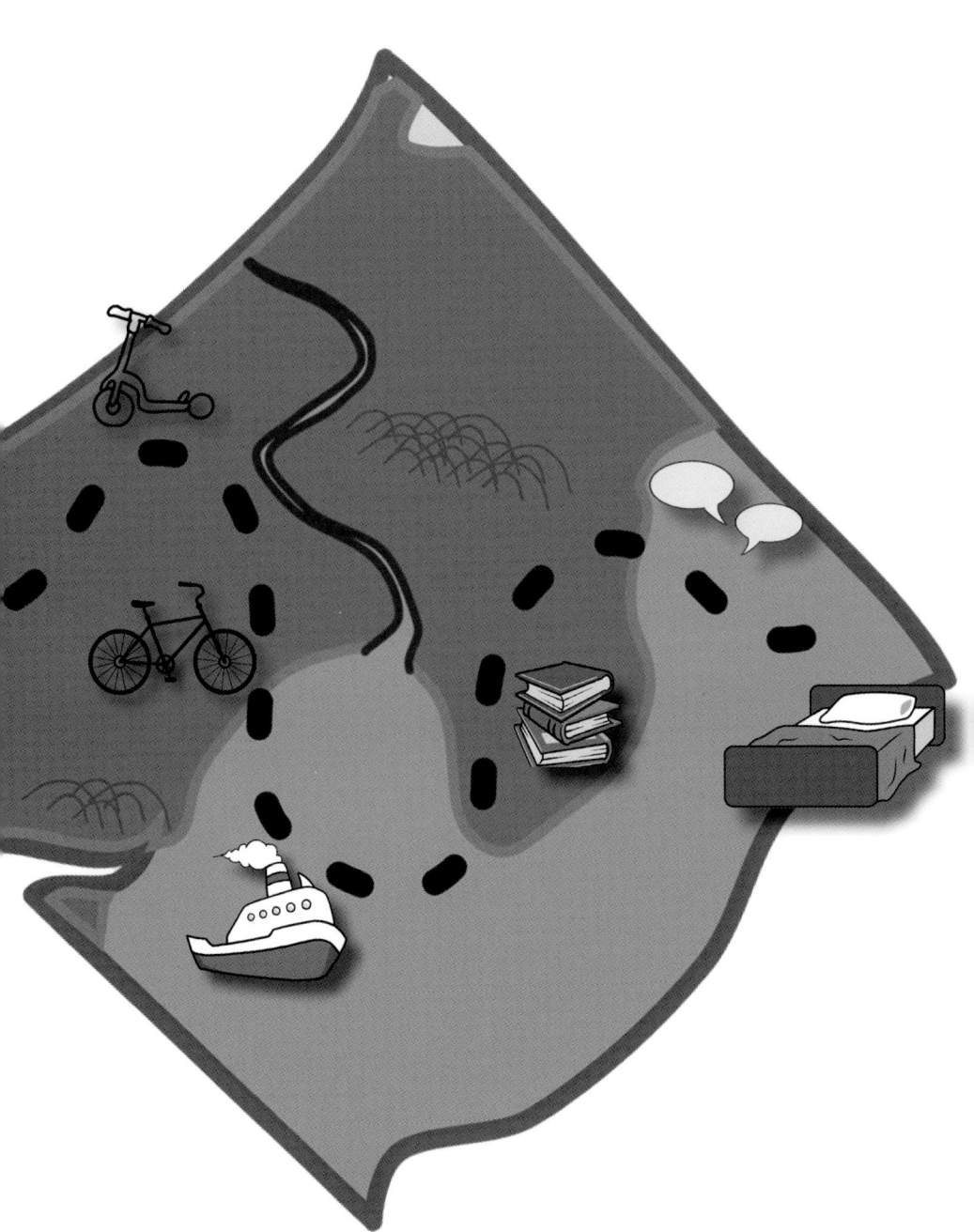

Daisy misses her friends and would love to be

somewhere in the sun with them having fun, but she had

a cold before Easter so for now she is happy to commune

with nature in her garden, and take it easy for a while.

Just For Now

I've got plenty of homework and things to get on with but mainly I'm missing my friends. I've not been feeling well but to be quite honest I'm glad that I have the chance at the moment to rest and *to lie sometimes on the grass under trees…watching the clouds float across the sky*[1] to get well and strong so I can be out there again with all of them when this thing all ends.

If I could be anywhere right now I'd be on a beach in Greece. Lots of white sand, smooth and soft, sparkling in the sun *in every grain of sand there is a story of the earth*[2]. We'd be there together just being lazy. The sky would be clear and the water see-through like crystal. The waves would crash but not too loudly. My beach is not going to be super noisy!

There will be birds *Come, on wings of joy we'll fly,* those tiny ones you hardly ever see *To where my bower hangs on high*, the ones that sing and the ones that talk *Come, and make thy calm retreat* but not so much that they are super annoying! There will be sausages cooking on the barbecue *Among green leaves and blossoms sweet*[3] and the taste of sea salt on your tongue.

That's where I'll be when this is done.

---

1   from 'The Pleasures of Life' by John Lubbock (1887)
2   from 'Silent Spring' by Rachel Carson (1962)
3   from 'The Birds' by William Blake (1800)

Flo held her new skates up in the air for me to see. She can't wait to get out there and try them out properly on the ground.

New Blades

Slamm... chu... kerrr... forward, balance, lean, but not like you're going to look down or dive into a swimming pool or anything like that *Tchuuuu... prrrrrr...* before we went on lockdown my dad gave me these new roller blades and I learned a new trick that I haven't been able to show anyone yet and I can't even practice it now because we are not allowed to be at the skatepark and I want to do inline not online skating I want to be out there jumping over the kerbs and whizzing round corners *Pchewwwwww!!!* and going up and down ramps and bouncing down steps and one day I'll even know how to ride along walls and twist in the air without falling off and I love how it sounds the rubber on wheels the way it whooshes and whirs when it rubs against surfaces like a rough engine rumble or an ocean roar or a great weight being rolled over gravel and sand and I had a dream that all my old shoes had turned into skates and that's when I woke up and remembered how great it is that I have these to go out with when lockdown is over and we're out of isolation and I can go over and show my dad everything I've learned since he last saw me.

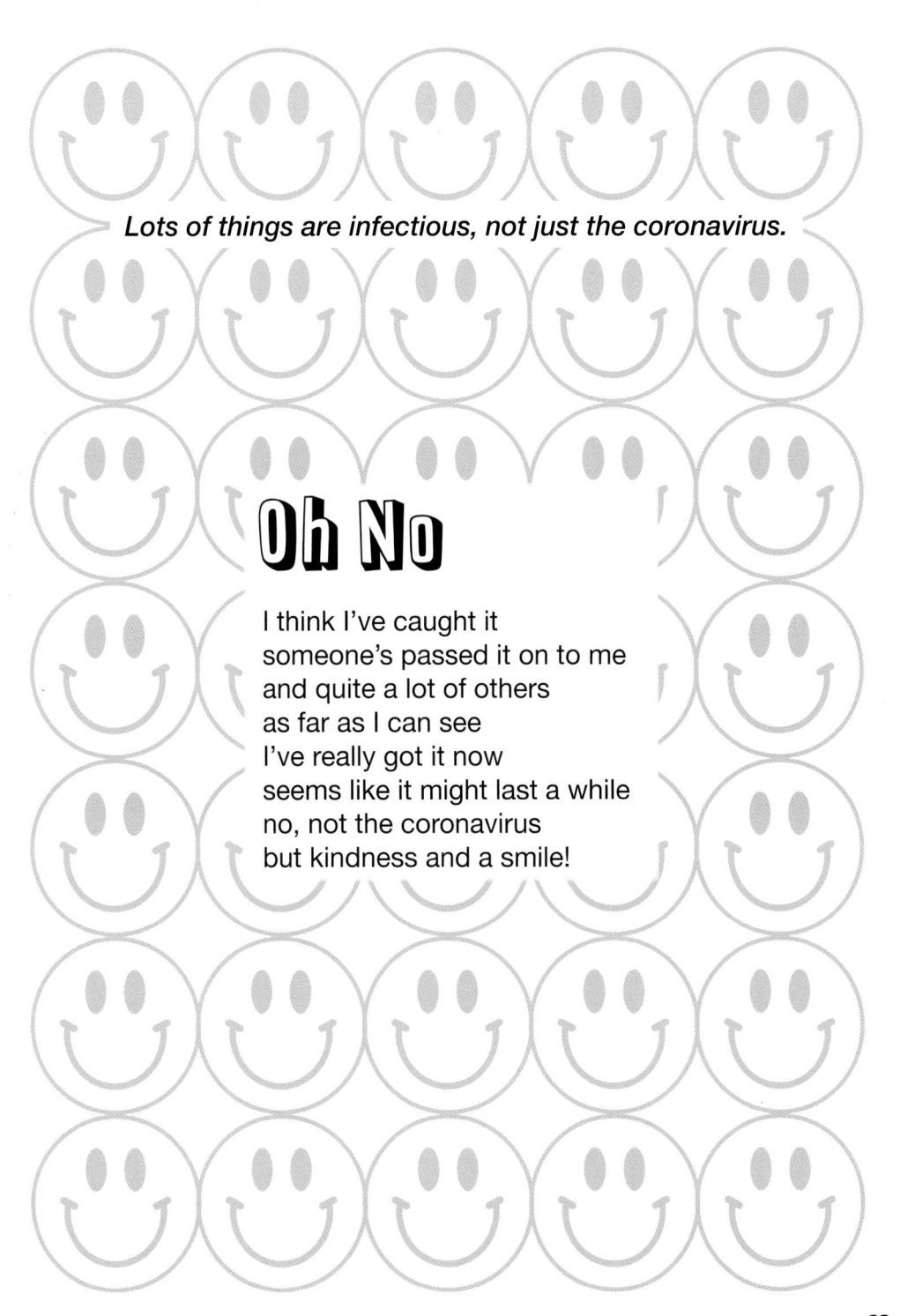

Lots of things are infectious, not just the coronavirus.

Oh No

I think I've caught it
someone's passed it on to me
and quite a lot of others
as far as I can see
I've really got it now
seems like it might last a while
no, not the coronavirus
but kindness and a smile!

Who Makes History?

Image by LoggaWiggler from Pixabay

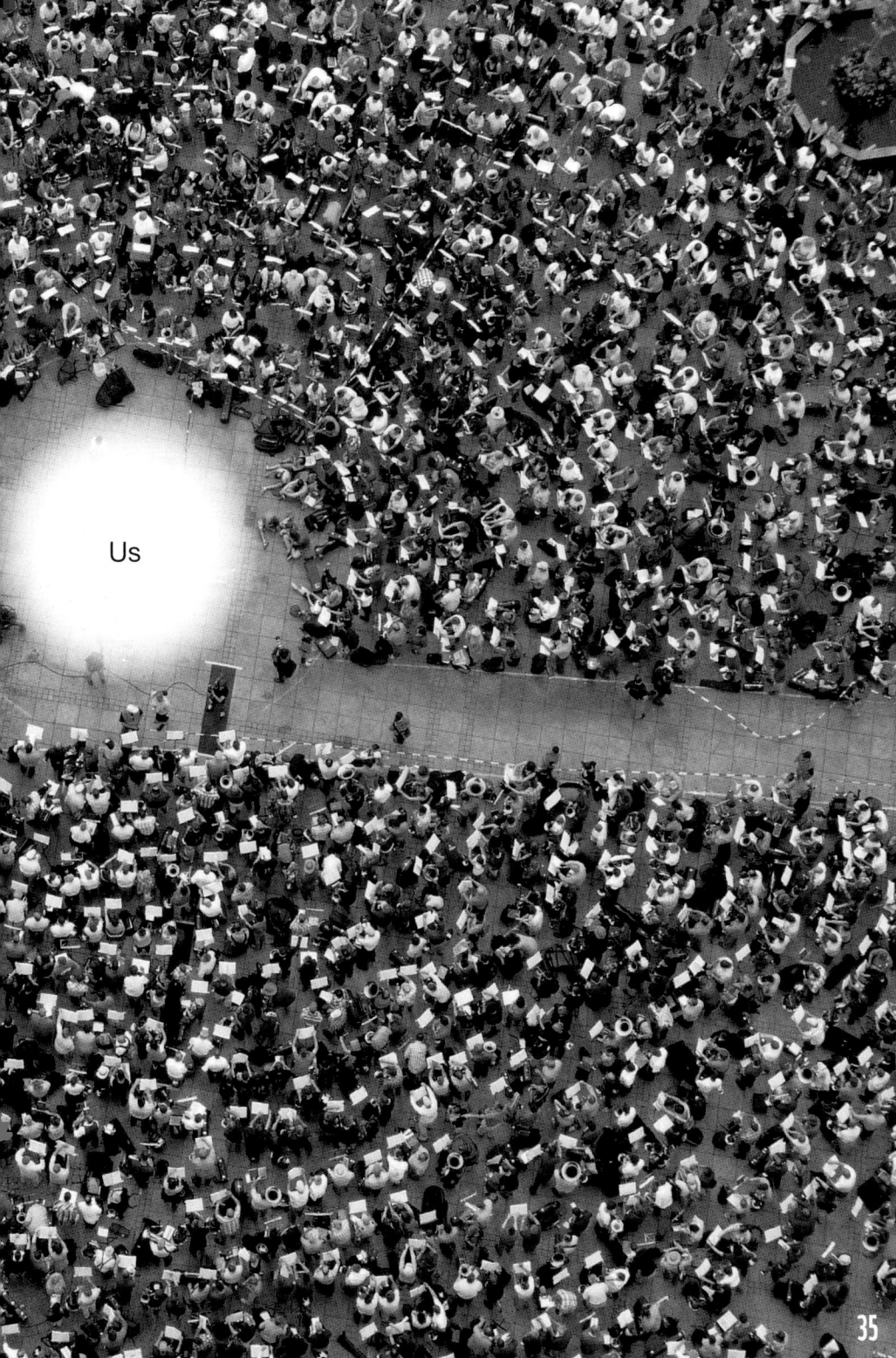

Hannah, age 13, lives opposite some playing fields called The Rec. There's a tennis court, a cricket pitch and a football field. During lockdown none of it is being used. That doesn't stop Hannah dreaming.

Fantasy Football

If I could go anywhere to do anything right now
I'd be playing team sports with my friends. Football!
Not anywhere far or special or weird,
just The Rec near my house, you can see it from here.
A friendly match (though we'd still win!)
If you're around, and want to, please come and join in.
I'll order some kit, Neon Orange, for the game.
We'll have a barbecue after, just drinks at half time.
Kick-off's at 10:30 so there'll be time for chilling
A lie-down on the grass if the weather is willing.
I'm sure it'll be sunny, but even if it's not,
I'll be happy with friends because they are all I've got.
They're the most precious thing in my life right now,
and I'm missing them so much, I can't tell you how.
I'll schedule the game soon, for a Saturday morning,
don't worry I'll make sure you all have good warning.
I'll invite everyone from home, and away.
We'll score loads of goals but at the end of the day,
we're not after victory, just playing the game.
We're not after special, only more of the same.
Normal is normal, that's what I love best
just being together with all of the rest.
And in case you're in doubt as to who you should cheer for
We're the *Rec-Lass Oranges* – football's what we're here for.

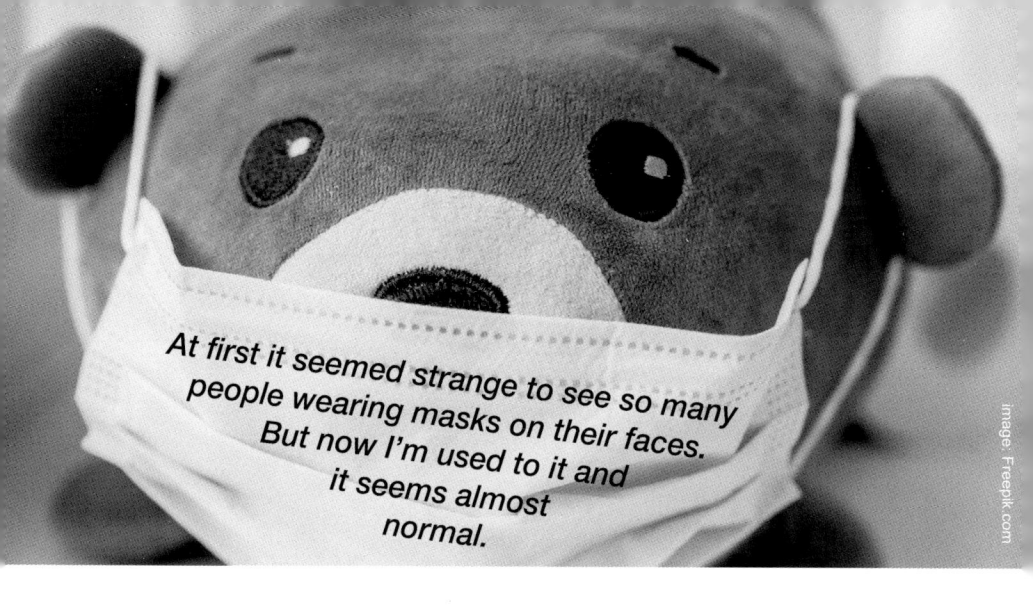

At first it seemed strange to see so many people wearing masks on their faces. But now I'm used to it and it seems almost normal.

Isn't It Odd

how things we once were convinced were good
like going outside as much as you could
or visiting relatives you know you should
are now not allowed and considered quite rude

Isn't it strange how we used to get mad
pretending that going to school made us sad –
we wanted more time at home than we had
but now when it re-opens we'll be so glad!

Isn't it funny how we used to want hoods
to pull over our heads and be cool dudes
and now we're covering our faces instead
making masks from paper, scarves or snoods

I don't think I ever really understood
how kindness works to lift your mood
So until this lockdown gets reviewed
I'm trying to be nicer than I usually would!

Nicola, is the site manager at a primary school. It's been no less busy for her during lockdown. She misses the children and wishes they could come back, but even in their absence she has had to be all things to all people.

Care Taker

We used to be called Caretakers
and to be honest, I think that
is what we should still be called.
Taking care is what we do,
looking after everyone's safety
the children, the staff, the school.

And now, the demands are constant.
The can I just have... I need more of...
hand sanitiser, paper towel, whatever!
Loo roll has become the new currency!
The role requires two of us, but I'm all
alone. Always on-site, never at home.

I'm a key-worker, we all are here. I'm
dead proud of all the staff, how quickly
they've learned how to adapt, now all
of us know the Corona Dance. Wash your
hands and keep your distance. And call
111 if you need medical assistance!

A kenning is a figure of speech dating back to Old English and Old Norse poetry – usually two words are combined to make a kind of metaphor for who or what you are describing.

Kennings For Nicola

She's a...
Cleaner-Upper, Care-Taker, Rule-Maker
Key-Holder, Stock-Checker, Code-Breaker
Problem-Solver, Light-Fixer, Sink-Unblocker
Alarm-Setter, Gate-Opener, Door-Locker
Everything-Doer, Miracle-Worker!

William is in Year 2. He told me he'd found the head of a peacock in his garden in London. He wishes everyone, including the foxes, would stop poaching, so endangered species can reproduce en masse!

During lockdown, there have been all sorts of amazing wildlife sightings. Here are just a few…

Animal Bonanza

Mountain goats in Llandudno
come down to see the town
Fallow deer in Romford
grazing on the lawn
Seabirds in Venice
enjoying the clear waters
Badgers at Sheffield station
making friends with otters
Sika deer in Nara
roaming freer than ever
Ducks in Paris
on the Rue de Sevres
Geese in Adana
sunbathing on the beach
Sheep in Turkey
parading down the streets
Pumas in Santiago
on the hunt for food
Monkeys in New Delhi
eating bananas on the road
Peacocks in Dubai
window-shopping in the Mall
slow worms in the compost
slithering over walls
Flamingos in Mumbai
a flock of lockdown-pink
Pelicans crossing London
real ones… I think!

One day in the future, you might get asked 'What was it like, living in the time of the coronavirus?' Keeping a journal during

Diary of William

A Collection of the most materiall occurrances and transactions in Public Affairs since One Hundred and Sixty Three and a Half Million years Ago, untill June, 2020, serving as a most usefull diurnall for future satisfaction and information during the time of ye Pandemick

Volume One

Published in London
Anno Domini 2020

lockdown can be a good way of remembering your ideas, thoughts, and the discoveries you are making right now.

Chapter One

Zoom is one of the many new ways to see people. I like pork crackling, I eat it loads. We had a VE day party on our road and someone made goose crackling. And cake. I found the severed head of a peacock in my garden. There have been others too. Pigeons. Once we camped all night in my garden. A fox came right up to the tent door. I think it is the foxes killing the birds. There's less pollution now, but it is still a problem. I think we should only be using cars if we need to. The Allosaurus lived 163.5 million years ago. Allosaurus means 'different lizard.' In 1671 an adventurer called Thomas Blood tried to steal the crown jewels from the Tower of London. He nearly succeeded. But not quite.

We are getting asked many questions during this lockdown. Here are some I've been hearing a lot...

Have You Washed Your Hands?

Have you washed your hands?
Have you washed your hands?
I know you're sick of hearing this
but have you washed your hands?

Is it Thursday yet?
Is it Thursday yet?
I want to clap the carers
Is it Thursday yet?

Can we chalk on the pavement?
Can we chalk on the pavement?
I want to thank the bin men
Can we chalk on the pavement?

Does Grandpa have an iPhone?
Does Grandpa have an iPhone?
I want to see him talking
Does Grandpa have an iPhone?

When is it the school holidays?
When is it the school holidays?
We're not going anywhere
When is it the school holidays?

Have you washed your hands?
Have you washed your hands?
I know you're sick of hearing this
but have you washed your hands?

"Have you washed your hands? Is it Thursday yet? Can we chalk on the pavement? Does Grandpa have an iPhone? When is it the school holidays? Have you washed your hands?"

Ela, Sami and Mario are all in Year 1. I asked all three of them...

What Is The Best Thing About Coming To School During Lockdown?

"I get to have a packed lunch"

"I'm more popular"

"I learn lots of stuff"

Tanka is a Japanese word meaning 'short poetry'. A tanka is a poem of five lines and thirty-one syllables (5-7-5-7-7) and no punctuation!

Daily Routine (A Tanka)

wake take temperature
wash hands with soap and water
try not to touch face
remember to bring packed lunch
and pocket sanitiser

SCHOOL TIMETABLE

Monday	wake take temperature / wash hands with soap and water / try not to touch face / remember to bring packed lunch / and pocket sanitiser
Tuesday	wake take temperature / wash hands with soap and water / try not to touch face / remember to bring packed lunch / and pocket sanitiser
Wednesday	wake take temperature / wash hands with soap and water / try not to touch face / remember to bring packed lunch / and pocket sanitiser
Thursday	wake take temperature / wash hands with soap and water / try not to touch face / remember to bring packed lunch / and pocket sanitiser
Friday	wake take temperature / wash hands with soap and water / try not to touch face / remember to bring packed lunch / and pocket sanitiser

Adem is in Year 4. He cares about ecology. He'd like to see real changes in the world after the pandemic.

All It Takes Is A Little Thought

If I made the rules
there'd be way more bins
no more littering in the ocean

Turtles eat plastic
it gets in their lungs
and causes extreme vasomotion

We must take care of
ourselves and others
otherwise we will soon be extinct

I think the virus
can teach a lesson,
not to panic, but learn how to think!

Adem's father had an idea for a way to brighten things up during lockdown, and has got the whole family working on it.

Colouring The Bricks

One by one, we are colouring the bricks

we are colouring them all with chalk

Dad set us the challenge to fill them all in

on the wall and the path where we walk.

Bit by bit we are covering each one

we are covering over the black

Mum says that they'll call this the 'Rainbow House'

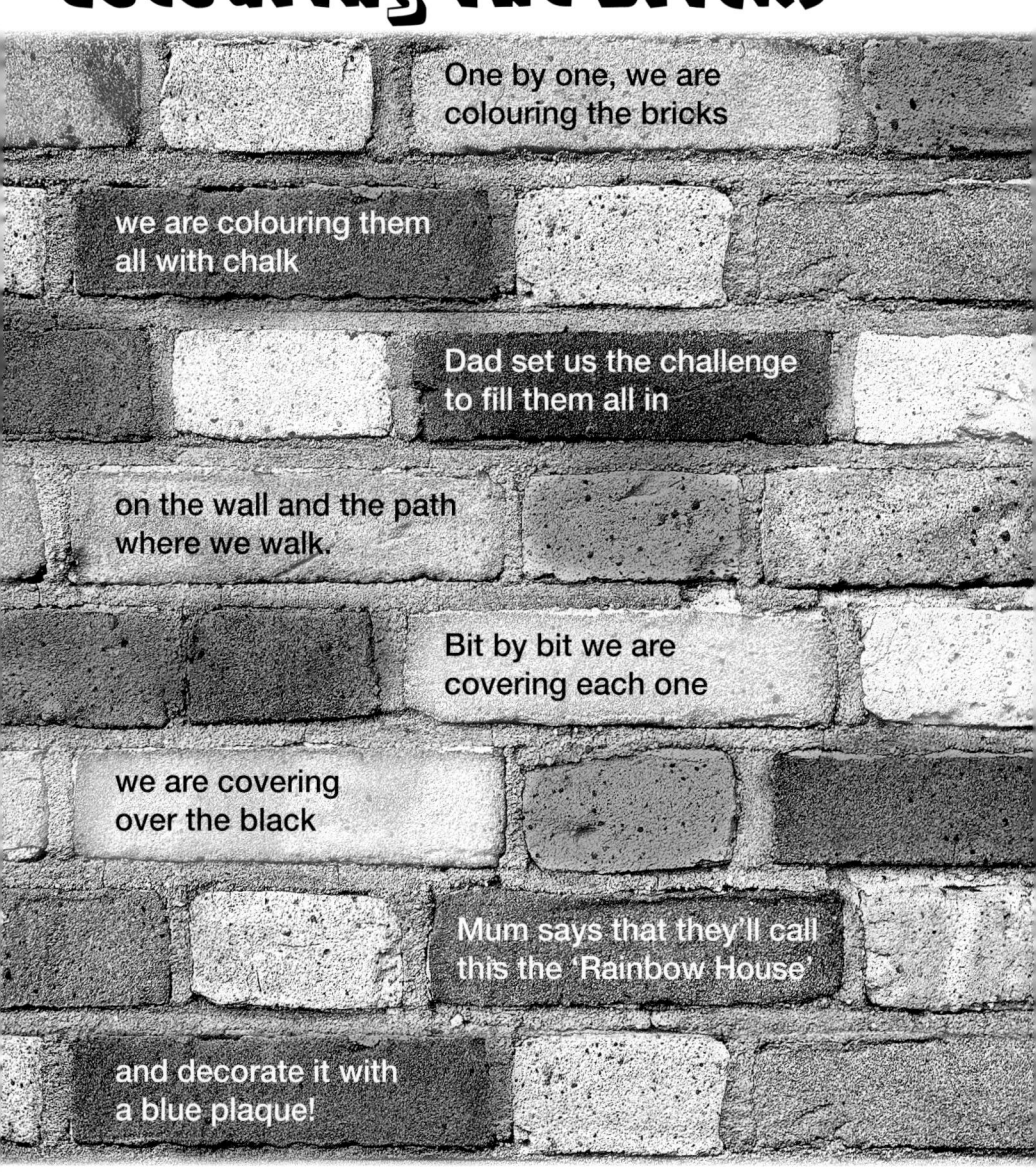

and decorate it with a blue plaque!

Arion teaches Year 4 but he has set this homework for everyone.

Life Lessons From A Teacher

Run, jump, play.
Fitness is important for everyone.

Communicate, call, write.
Keep in touch with family and friends.

Read, study, learn.
Make wherever you are your classroom.

Sharon is a school office manager by day. During lockdown she also has become a bit of a night owl and has made some great astronomical discoveries.

Sharon says it's hard to believe, looking up at all that beauty, that people are suffering so much down here.

SpaceX

What's this?
A line of shining birds in flight?
A giant string of Christmas lights?
No! It's a train of Starlink satellites!

Sharon's Sky At Night

Pink moon, Flower moon, Supermoon
Evening star, Earth's sister, Venus
Bull Hunter, jewel of Heaven, Orion
Great Bear, Big Dipper, Ursa Major
North Star, guiding light, Polaris
Brightest star, Dog Star, Sirius
Crouching Lion, spring bringer, Leo
Falling star, wishing star, new hope

Audrey is 5. She's looking forward to a time when she doesn't have to go to hospital so much anymore.

When I Am Well Again

First of all, I would go to the park
afterwards, maybe the moon
I'd ride on my scooter till it gets dark
but for now, I'll stay in my room

I used to be on the Lion Ward
with loads of toys and playthings
but now I stay in the Pelican Ward
because of Covid-19

Some of the children in Lion Ward
have leukaemia just like me
all of the children in Pelican Ward
are staying in quarantine

I have a good view from my window
the garden, the road, and the park
I play with my brother, William
and like doing lots of art!

I miss all my friends in Reception
I'd like to see them quite soon
we could go on our scooters together
and jump up and down on the moon

Now that there's not so much traffic noise outside you can hear birds singing most of the time! This morning I was woken by one that seemed to be telling me to get out of bed even though it was only 4.30am and the sun wasn't up yet.

The blackbird and the nightingale are both known for singing even when it is still dark.

Round The Clock Song

The blackbird
calls
like Mum
in the morning
saying
come on then
come on then
get up sleepyhead!

Nightingale
hums
like Gran
in the evening
singing
day is done
day is done
I'm going to bed.

Brooke is in Year 3. She's hoping that after coronavirus is gone, there will only be respect, kindness and friendship in the world. She's worried though that there might still be social distancing when it's her birthday in the summer and even if she does have a party no one will come or if they do, they will have to stay 2 metres apart!

Okay I said to Brooke, let's not worry about that now. Let's plan for the perfect birthday. What time will you get up?

Unicorn Magic

Brooke   Very early. I don't want to be late for my birthday.
Me   Right! What will you do first when you wake up?

Brooke	Jump out of my bed, it's a bunk bed, I'll jump from the top! I have a bunk bed in my room even though it's only one person, me, in it!
Me	What will you do then?
Brooke	Go and jump on my mum and dad's bed. I'll jump on them and say 'It's my BIRTHDAY!!!!'
Me	Great. Will they wake up?
Brooke	No. My mum doesn't like to get up early. She'll say 'go away!'
Me	But it's your birthday!
Brooke	I know. So I'll jump some more.
Me	And then they'll wake up.
Brooke	Yes.
Me	So are you going to have a party?
Brooke	Yes, I'll have it at my house.
Me	Good. What kind of party?
Brooke	Well my last party was Hawaiian. This time I'll have a Unicorn party.
Me	With Unicorn hats?
Brooke	Yes and a Unicorn cake.
Me	Unicorn cups and plates?
Brooke	Unicorn everything! Unicorns are really nice. I have a Unicorn in my room and I think she comes alive at night.
Me	Really? What does she do?
Brooke	She lets me climb on her back and then she flies me places. I hold on to her horn so I don't fall off.
Me	Will she come to your party?
Brooke	Yes!
Me	And sing Happy Birthday to you?
Brooke	No. We'll sing a Unicorn song together.
Me	You mean like this one?
	On the day that Brooke was born, *there came a magic Unicorn* *And now that Brooke is turning eight,* *she's here to help Brooke celebrate!*
Brooke	Yup!!

Evie is in Year 6. The worst thing for her about lockdown is not getting to see all people she loves and having to miss special days with her family. At the beginning of April it was her grandma's 76th birthday and all she could do was stand outside the house where her grandma lives and talk to her from there. What's the point of that, asked Evie?

Okay, I said to Evie, let's wind the clock back three weeks and make it the perfect birthday for your grandma. Let's start in the morning. What will you do first?

Virtually There

I'll call her and say Happy Birthday. Then I'll make a cake with rainbow layers of positivity and decorate the top with strawberries. Grandma's favourite. It will take hours to bake.

I'll dress up in my blue and coral dress. Grandma likes bright colours, especially those that remind her of the sea or the sky. She likes nail polish too – I'll look for something iridescent.

Grandma told me once that if you wish on a star it can turn into a diamond for your pocket. I'll make a bracelet from the moon and turn my heart into a locket with a picture of me inside.

I'll make a banner that stretches as far as the wind can blow so that when Grandma stands by her window she'll hear the collared doves outside singing the message that's written on it.

Whoo-hoo hoo hoo-hoo
Whoo-hoo hoo hoo-hoo
Happy Birthday dear Grandma
Happy Birthday to you!

Happy Birthday Grandma!

Alex, a Year 6 teacher said, 'We were all looking forward to our last few months together in Year 6. We would normally have a

The Show Must Go On

So, while we're all sitting alone in our rooms,
why not do our Year 6 production by Zoom?
There's nothing to do and nowhere to play
and it's boring to sit here alone every day.

I know I'm your teacher, but I, too, get the hump.
If I'm bored for too long, I become a real Grump
Remember that Cat who stepped onto the mat?
Remember the way he just barged in like that?

Now I know we all have to behave in Year 6,
I'm not seriously suggesting we do all those tricks
with the fish in the bowl, the cup and the cake
the milk in the dish, the toys and the rake.

But… just say each one of us opened a box
unhooked the hooks and undid the locks…
Just say that inside every box was the same:
Two Things that jumped out and wanted a game!

What are they up to, Thing Two and Thing One?
What exactly is their idea of fun?
To fly a kite in the hall and make a big mess?
To jump on the bed, or ruin a dress?

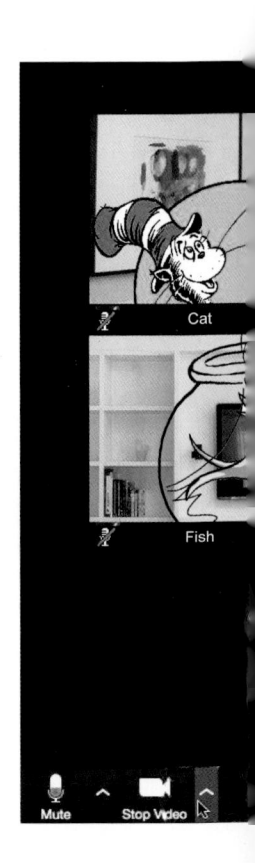

final production. This year I was thinking about **The Cat in the Hat...'**

If you were a Thing, and it was your mission
to do what you fancied, without permission,
what will it be, Thing One or Thing Two?
Which one would you be, and what would you do?

When you've got your ideas, send them to me
And we'll make this production happen, you'll see
Our final production will be a sensation
And to think that we managed it in isolation!!!

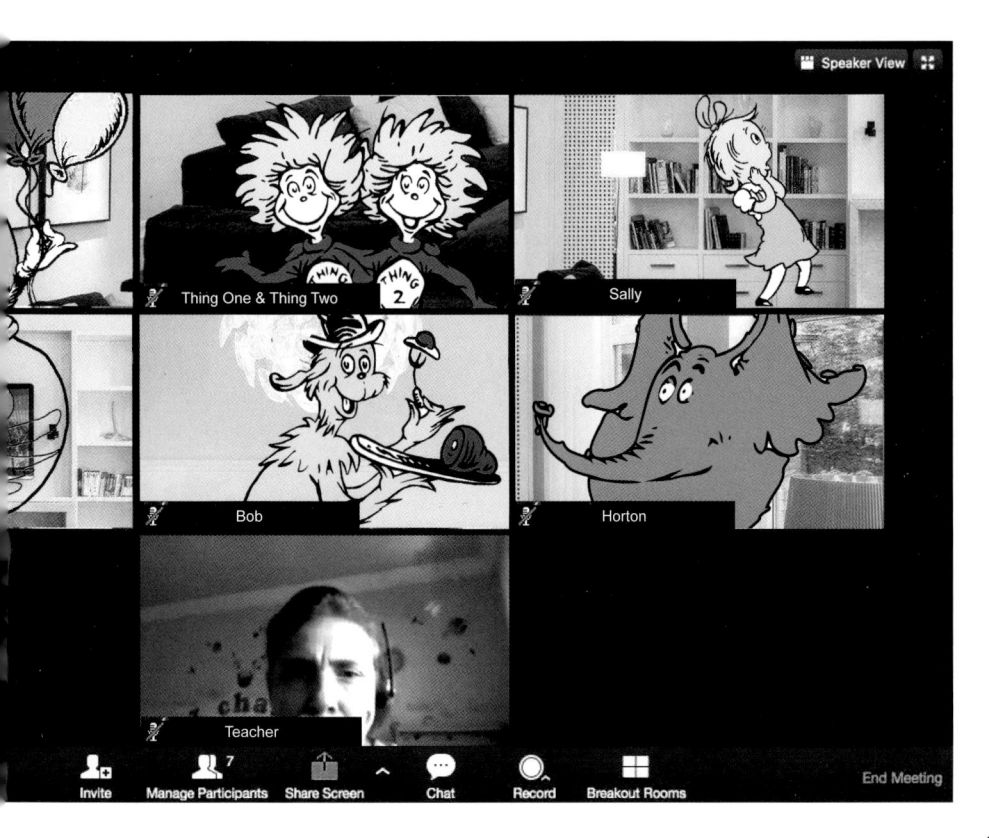

Alfie is missing seeing his dad, and the rest of his family. His perfect day would to be with everyone all together. His nan, auntie, mum, dad, uncles, cousins…

Perfect Day

It's a pizza-eating, film-watching
family-snuggling, cake-baking
crumb-dropping, drink-spilling
uncle-teasing, joke-telling
Dad-yawning, cousin-chilling
auntie-tickling, Nan-giggling
Mum-laughing, everyone-saying
'Please can this go on forever day'.

there would be over ten of them! Alfie says they could go to his Nan's because she has a big living room. They'd order in pizza and watch loads of films.

Photo by Abdulaziz AlAbdullah on Unsplash

Making A Meal Of Pizza

I like ham and pineapple,
Dad always has pepperoni.
Nan likes hers with everything
and takes the menu to show me.

I wish that there were pizzas
we could order for pudding too
I'd have the lemon drizzle
with gallons of chocolate goo!

Even if you are a head teacher, it's hard to keep everything going during lockdown.

Ahoy There, A Word From Your Captain

We're sailing this ship with a much-reduced crew
we're keeping afloat
but we're struggling too

We all have days when we're tired or bored
days when it feels like
we're being ignored

We're doing our best to keep spirits up
but being at sea
is hard when school's shut.

Exercise too has been scarce for a while
whatever happened
to the Daily Mile?

Once back on dry land I'll run a tight ship
no lazing around,
it's time to get fit!

So avast me hearties, hoist up your sails
Hard Work and Patience
these too will prevail!

Headteacher's Office ←

Carterhatch Juniors

A manifesto is a public declaration of aims and intentions and ideas for a better future. J'Ziah is in Year 4 – this is his.

J'Ziah's Manifesto For The New World

Say there's a new world
when this one has vanished
the virus all finished
lockdown abolished.

I'm gonna make certain
the Earth keeps on turning
and all of the children
get on with their learning.

We'll have to make changes
things can't stay the same
so hold on to your dreams
that's the name of the game.

When Covid-19 is
not here to plague us
we should be allowed
to go to Las Vegas

and visit the places
where relatives are
like Boston and Kenya
and Nigeria!

Too many have suffered
it's sad but it's true
though the sun is still shining
and the sky is still blue.

Say there's a new world
when we've conquered this thing
we'll run, and we'll play
and we'll dance, and we'll sing!

Cocoon

Caterpillar-like
Contained in a chrysalis
Metamorphosing

Transforming ourselves
Soon to be spreading our wings
Like a butterfly